Josephine Franklin

Little Bessie, the Careless Girl

Or Squirrels, Nuts, and Water-Cresses

Josephine Franklin

Little Bessie, the Careless Girl
Or Squirrels, Nuts, and Water-Cresses

ISBN/EAN: 9783337061647

Printed in Europe, USA, Canada, Australia, Japan

Cover: Foto ©Andreas Hilbeck / pixelio.de

More available books at **www.hansebooks.com**

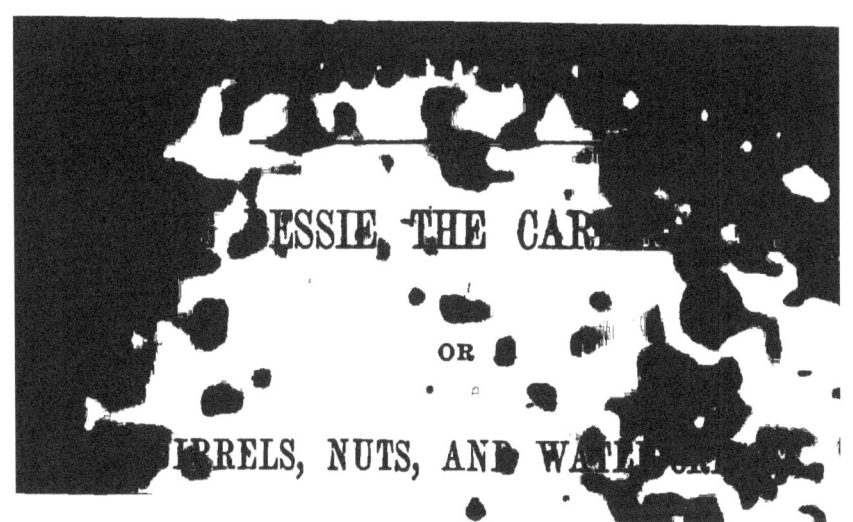

ESSIE, THE CAR

OR

IRRELS, NUTS, AND WAT

BY

JOSEPHINE FRANKLIN,

AUTHOR OF "NELLY AND HER FRIENDS," "NELLY'S
SCHOOL-DAYS," "NELLY AND HER BOAT," ETC.

BOSTON:
PUBLISHED BY BROWN AND TAGGARD,
25 AND 29 CORNHILL.
1861.

RIVERSIDE, CAMBRIDGE:

STEREOTYPED AND PRINTED BY H. O. HOUGHTON.

CONTENTS.

. LITTLE BESSIE;

OR,

SQUIRRELS, NUTS, AND WATERCRESSES.

CHAPTER I.

GOING NUTTING.

BESSIE was the only child of a poor widow. The mother and daughter lived alone together in a small house, about half a mile from Nelly's home.

Bessie's father died when she was quite young, so young that she did not remember him. There was a portrait of him, which her mother kept in her top bureau drawer in her own room. Occasionally

the little girl was allowed to look at it.
It made her feel very sad to do so, and the
tears rose in her eyes whenever she
thought of what her mother must have
suffered in so great a loss. In the hard
task which fell to that mother of support-
ing herself and her child, she did not murmur. Before her husband's death, she had
lived in very comfortable circumstances,
but this did not unfit her to work for her
living afterwards.

She gathered and sent fruit to market
from her little place, she made butter and
sold it to whomever cared to buy, she knit
stockings for her neighbors' children, and,
every winter, quilted to order at least one
dozen patchwork counterpanes, with wonderful yellow calico suns in their centre.
By these means she contrived to keep out
of debt, and amass a little sum besides.

At the commencement of our story, however, a severe fit of illness had so wasted
her strength and devoured her little means,
that the poor widow felt very much dis-
couraged. The approach of winter filled
her with dread, for she knew that it would
be to her a time of great suffering.

Still, feeble as she was, she managed to
continue, but very irregularly, Bessie's
reading and writing lessons. Bessie was
not a promising scholar; she liked to do
any thing in the world but study. She
would look longingly out of the window a
dozen times in the course of a single lesson, and when her mother reproved her
by rapping her rather smartly on the head
with her thimble, Bessie would only laugh,
and say she guessed her skull must be
thick, for the lesson *would not* get through,
and the thimble did not hurt a bit!

Bessie, and Nellie Brooks, of whom my readers have heard in the former stories of this series, were very much attached to each other. Bessie was younger than Nellie, but that did not stand in the way of their affection. Nellie, imperfect as she was herself, used to try sometimes to teach Bessie how to improve her wild ways. Bessie would listen and listen, as grave as a cat watching a rat hole, but her little eyes would twinkle in the midst of the reproof, and she would burst into a merry shout, and say, "I do declare, Nell, it isn't any use at all to talk to me about being any better. I'm like the little birds; they're born to fly and sing, and I'm born to be horrid and naughty, and dance, and cry, and laugh, just when I shouldn't, — there! I can't be good, anyway. Sometimes I try, and mother looks as pleased as can be, and all at once, before I know it, I flounder straight into mischief again."

One beautiful autumn day, Nellie and Bessie went nutting in the woods. Each of the little girls had a basket on her arm, and Bessie had a bag besides; for they had great hopes of coming home heavily loaded. It was early in October. The leaves of the trees had begun to fall, but those that remained were bright with many colors, the crimson of the maple trees particularly, making the whole woods look gay. A soft, golden mist, such as we only see at this season of the year, hung over every thing, and veiled even the glitter of a little river which flowed past the village and coursed onward to the ocean.

At first the children met with very little success. The first few nut-trees they encountered had evidently been visited by some one before.   The marks of trampling feet were visible on the damp ground beneath, and the branches had been stripped in such rude haste as to take away both the leaves and the fruit.

" We'll meet better luck further back in the woods," said Nell; " this is too near home.   The village people can come here too easily for us to expect to find any thing."

They walked further on in very good spirits, climbing over rocks when they came to them, and swinging their empty baskets in time to snatches of songs which they sang together.   They had gone in this way about a mile, when suddenly Bessie stopped, and fixed her eyes searchingly on something near them in the grass.

" What is the matter ? " said Nellie.

" Hush, hush ! " said Bessie, softly, "don't

speak for a minute till I see! It's an animal!"

"A bear?" exclaimed Nellie, in some
alarm, quite unmindful of Bessie's request
for silence, for Nelly was a little bit of a
coward, and had a firm belief in all woods
being full of wild animals. As she spoke,
the noise seemed to startle whatever the
creature was that Bessie was watching, for
it ran quickly among the dried leaves that
strewed the grass, and bounded on a high
rock not far distant.

"There!" said Bessie, in a vexed tone,
"you've frightened him away. We might
have tracked him to his hole if you had
kept still."

"I was afraid it was a bear," said Nelly,
half ashamed.

"A bear!" cried Bessie, in great scorn;
"I'd like to see a bear in *these* woods."

"Would you? *I* wouldn't," said Nelly.

"I mean — well — I mean there isn't a bear around here for hundreds of miles. That was a squirrel you frightened away. Didn't he look funny springing up there?"

"He's there now, looking at us. Don't you see his head sticking out of that bush? What bright eyes he has."

Bessie found that it was so. There was the squirrel's head, twisted oddly on one side, in order to get a good view of his disturbers. His keen eyes were fixed anxiously on them, as though to discover the cause of their intrusion. Presently he leaped on a branch of a shrub, and sat staring solemnly at them.

"It can't be a squirrel," said Bessie, "after all; its tail is not half bushy or long enough."

"It jumps like one," said Nellie, "and

its eyes and ears are just like a squirrel's too. See, it's gray and white!"

They approached slowly, the little animal permitting them to come quite close, and then the children saw that it was indeed a squirrel, but that its tail had, by some accident, been torn nearly half away.

"Perhaps it has been caught in a trap," suggested Nelly.

"Or in a branch of a tree," said Bessie. "Well, anyway, little Mr. Squirrel, we shall know you again if we meet you."

"I should say," exclaimed Nelly, "that there must be plenty of nuts somewhere near us, or that gray squirrel would not be likely to be here."

The two girls now set about searching for a hickory nut-tree, quite encouraged in the thought that their walk was to be rewarded at last. Nelly was right in her conjecture. It was not long before they recognized the well-known leaf of the species of tree of which they were in quest. A small group of them stood together, not far distant, and great was the delight of the children to find the ground beneath well strewed with nuts, some of them lying quite free from their rough outer shells, others only partially opened, while many of them were still in the exact state in which they hung upon the tree. Of course the former were preferred by the little nut gatherers, but it was found that as these did not fill the bag and baskets, it was necessary to shell some of the remainder. Accordingly, Bessie selected a large flat stone, as the scene of operation, and providing herself with another small one, as a hammer, she began pounding the unshelled nuts, and by these means accumulated a second store; Nelly gathering them, and making a pile beside her, ready to be denuded of their hard green coverings.

"There," triumphantly said Nelly, after a little while; "that dear little squirrel told the truth. Here is quite a pile of shells showing the mark of his teeth. See, Bessie, he has nibbled away the sides of all these, and eaten the meat. How neatly it is done, and what sharp little fangs he must have!"

The bag and baskets were soon filled, and the two children turned homeward. The day was a warm one for that season of the year, and their burdens were very hard to carry on that account. Many a time they paused on the path to put down the baskets and rest.

"I hope," said Nelly, "that when we get out to the open road, some wagon will

come along that will give us a lift. Who
would have thought that nuts could be so
heavy? I am so warm and *so* thirsty, I do
not know how to get along, and there isn't
a single brook about here that we can
drink out of."

"I'll tell you how we will fix it," said
Bessie. "I remember, last year, when I
came nutting, I saw a little house, a poor
little concern, — not half as nice as ours,
and dear knows that is poor enough, —
standing in the edge of the wood, about
half a mile below where we are now. We
can stop when we get there, and I will
go in and borrow a tin cup to drink out of
the well."

"A half mile!" echoed Nelly, in a tone
of weariness; "I don't believe we shall get
there in an hour, I am so very, very tired."

They walked on slowly, the peculiar

heaviness of the warm October day making each of them feel that to go nutting in such weather was very hard work. At last the little house presented itself. It was a poor place indeed. It was built of rough pine boards that had never been painted. A dog lay sleeping before the door, the upper half of which was open, and through which the sunshine poured into the room. The house stood, as Bessie had said, on the edge of the wood, large, fertile fields extending in the distance, on the opposite side from that by which the children had approached it.

"You knock," said Bessie, getting struck with a fit of shyness, as the two walked up the path to the door.

"No, *you*," said Nelly, "I don't know what to say." .

The dog got up, stretched himself, and

gave vent to a low growl, as he surveyed the new comers.

"Good fellow, nice fellow," said Bessie, coaxingly, putting out her hand towards him as she did so; but the good, nice fellow's growl deepened into a loud, savage bay. The children stood still, irresolute whether to retreat or not. Attracted by the noise, a pale, sickly girl about fifteen years of age, came to the door, and leaning over the lewer half which was shut, seemed by looking at them to ask what they wanted.

"Please," said Bessie, "would you mind lending me a tin dipper to drink out of at your well?"

"Haven't got any well," said the girl; "but you can drink out of the spring if you've a mind to. There it is, down by that log: it runs right from under it.

You'll find a mug lying 'long side. Do stop your noise, Tiger."

The children set down their baskets, and moved towards the spring very gladly. They found the mug, and each enjoyed a drink of the pure, cold water. While doing so, they observed that near the little barn at the rear of the house, a man was harnessing a sleek, comfortable looking horse to a market wagon, laden with cabbages and potatoes. The man was thin and white looking, and it seemed to the children as if the proper place for him were his bed. He did not see the visitors, but went on with his work. The girls having finished drinking, returned to the front door, over which still leaned the sickly girl.

"Much obliged to you," said Nelly, "it's a beautiful spring; clear and cold as ever I saw."

"'Tisn't healthy though," said the girl; "leastways, we think it's that that brings us all down with the fever every spring and fall."

"The fever!" echoed Bessie, "what fever?"

"The fever'n nager," replied the girl. "Mother is in bed with it now, and though father is getting ready to go to town to market, the shakin' is on him right powerful. I'm the only one that keeps about, and that is much as ever, too."

"What makes you drink it?" asked Bessie. "I wouldn't, if it made me so sick."

"Have to," said the girl, "there is no other water hereabouts."

"Can't your father *move?*" said Nelly.

The girl shook her head.

"Wouldn't he *like* to, if he could?" continued Nelly.

"I guess not," said the girl, "we mean to get used to it. We can't afford to move. Father , owns the place, and he has no chance to sell it. The farm is good, too. We raise the best cabbages and potatoes around here. Guess you've been nutting, haven't you?"

"Yes," said Bessie, with some pride, "we have those two baskets and this bag *full*."

"Is it much fun?" asked the girl pleasantly.

"Splendid," said Bessie; "don't you ever try it?"

"No; I'm always too sick in nut season — have the shakes. But I do believe I should like to some time. Are you two little girls going soon again?"

"I don't know," said Bessie, "may be so. If we do, shan't we stop and see if you are able to go along? Your house isn't much out of the way; we can stop just as well as not."

The pale girl looked quite gratified at these words of Bessie, but said that she didn't know whether the "shakes" would allow her.

"Well," said Bessie, "we will stop for you, anyway. My mother would say, I am sure, that the walk would do you good. Good-by. I hope you will all get better soon."

"Stop a moment," said the girl, "don't you live somewhere down by the Brooks' farm?"

"Yes," said Nelly, "that is my home, and Bessie lives only a little way beyond."

"I thought so," said the girl, smiling, "I think I've seen you when I have been riding by with father. He's going that way, now: wouldn't you like to get in the wagon with him? He will pass your house."

"Oh, I guess his load is heavy enough already," said Nelly.

"Nonsense," said the girl; "you just wait here, while I go ask him."

She darted off before they could detain her, and in a short time more, the horse and wagon appeared round the corner of the house, the man driving the fat horse (which, as far as the children could see, was the only fat living creature on the place), and the girl walking at the wagon side.

"There they are," the children heard her say, as she neared them.

The man smiled good naturedly, and bade Bessie and Nelly jump in. He arranged a comfortable seat for them on the board on which he himself sat.

"But isn't your load very heavy already, sir?" asked Nelly.

"Not a bit of it," said the farmer; "my horse will find it only a trifle, compared to what we usually take. It isn't full market day to-morrow is the reason. Jump in! jump in!"

The children needed no other bidding, but clambered up by the spokes of the great wheels and seated themselves, one on each side of the farmer, who took their nuts, and placed them safely back among his vegetables.

Then he cracked his whip, and called out, "Good-by, Dolly. I'll be home about eleven o'clock to-night. Take good care of your mother."

The next moment the little girls were in the road, going homeward as fast as the sleek horse could carry them.

CHAPTER II.

THE RIDE HOME.

"So you've been nutting, eh?" said Mr. Dart (for that was the farmer's name), looking first on one side of him and then on the other, where his two companions sat.

"Yes, sir," said Nelly, "and we have had real good luck too. Only see how full our baskets are."

"Dolly told me you were going to stop for her some time, to go nutting with you," said the farmer, turning round as he spoke, and putting a cabbage that was jolting out of the wagon back into its place. "I am glad of that: I hope she will be able to accompany you. If you should

chance to come on one of her well days, I
guess she will."

" Well days, sir ? " asked Bessie.

" Yes; she has the fever'n nager pretty
bad, and that brings her a sick day and a
well day, by turns. It's the natur' of the
disease."

" What ! sick *every* other day ! " cried
Bessie; — " well, if that is not too bad !
And she seems so good too. Why, we
owe this ride to her."

" Yes," said the farmer, " Dolly is a pretty good little girl. Never had much trouble with Dolly in all her life. She's always
willin' to help round the house as much as
she can, and now that her mother is down
with the nager, I couldn't get along without her, anyway. In the summer time
Dolly makes garden with the best of us.
Many is the field she's sowed with grain,

after I've ploughed it up. Half of these ere cabbages Dolly cut and put in the wagon herself. You see that little basket back in the corner?"

The children looked back in the wagon, and there, sure enough, was a small covered basket, jolting around among the potatoes.

"That's Dolly's water cresses," said Mr. Dart. "I haven't taken a load to market for the last month without Dolly's basket of watercresses. She gathers them herself, down in our meadow, where the ground is wet and soft, and where they thrive like every thing. They seem to be getting poor now, and I don't believe Doll will be able to pick many more this year. Why, the money that girl has made off them cresses is wonderful. I always hand it right over to her, and she puts it by to save against a time of need. Cresses sell just like wild-fire in our market-place, — I mean, of course, fine ones like my Dolly's are in their prime."

"Cresses," said Bessie, with growing interest, "do people really pay money for *cresses?* Why, the field back of our house is full of 'em! They have great, thick, green leaves, and they look as healthy as possible."

"Do they?" said the farmer, smiling at her kindly; "well, then I can just tell you your folks are fortunate. They ought to sell 'em and make money out of them."

"I wish we could," said Bessie, clasping her hands at the thought, "how glad mother would be if we could! Mother is sick, sir, and cannot do all the work she used, to earn money."

"Ah," said the farmer, with a look of concern; "I am sorry to hear that, my little girl. I know what it is to be sick, and have sick folks about me. What's the matter? has she got the nager too?"

"No, sir," said Bessie, "we don't have that down our way. I don't know what *does* ail mother. She sort o' wastes away and grows thin and pale."

"Like enough it's the nager," said the farmer; "there is nothing like it for making a body thin and pale."

"That's Bessie's house," cried Nelly, as a sudden turn in the road revealed their two homes, at the foot of the hill, "that white one with the smoke curling out of the left hand chimney."

"And a nice little place it is too," said the farmer. "I pass right by it almost every day, and sometimes in the middle of the night, when all little girls are in their beds and asleep."

Bessie looked at the kind-hearted farmer, and wondered to herself what could bring him so near her home in the night-time. As her thoughts by this time were pretty well filled with what he called the " nager," she concluded that it must be for the purpose of getting the doctor for himself and his family. The farmer, however, who seemed fond of talking, soon undeceived her.

" You see," he began, " that it is a very long drive from my house to town, say eight miles, at the least, and when I start as I have to-day, about sundown, it takes me, with a heavy load, generally, till half past eight o'clock to get to the market. Well, then I unload, and sell out to a regular customer I have, a man who keeps a stand of all sorts of vegetables, and who generally buys them over night in this way. Then I turn round and come back. It is often eleven o'clock when I reach home and go to bed. Sometimes, again, according to the orders I have from town, Dobbin and I start — "

" Dobbin?" interrupted Bessie, " is Dobbin the horse, sir ? "

The farmer nodded smilingly, and continued, " Dobbin and I start at five o'clock in the morning, and we go rattling into market, just in time to have the things hurriedly sorted and in their places, before the buyers begin to throng about the stalls. I stop there a while, but I get home before noon, and Dolly always has my dinner ready to rest me, while Dobbin eats his to rest *him*."

3

"I wish Dolly could go to our school," said Nelly, after a pause. "Miss Milly, our teacher, is so good to us all. She lives in this little house that we are passing."

The farmer looked round at the school-house, and Nelly thought she heard him sigh as he did so. "Dolly is a smart girl, and a nice girl," said he, gravely, "but I am afraid her mother and I can't give her much book larnin'. Wish I could: but times are hard and money scarce. Dolly knows how to read and write, and I guess she will have to be content. Her health isn't strong, either, and she couldn't stand study."

"Here we are, sir, this is our house," cried Nelly, as the wagon neared the farmhouse gate. "I'm very much obliged to you for my lift."

The farmer handed down her basket of

nuts, and told her she was quite welcome.
Bessie called out good-by, and the farmer
drove on again. A short distance brought
them to Bessie's house. As she in her turn
was getting down, Mr. Dart asked her if
she had any objections to show him the
water-cress field of which she had spoken.
Bessie was delighted to do it, so Dobbin
was tied to a tree, and the little girl led
the way to the back of the house.

"Does the field belong to your mother?"
asked the farmer.

"Yes, sir," said Bessie, "this house and
the garden and the wet meadow where
the watercresses grow, mother owns them
all. She's sick now, as I told you, sir, and
oftentimes she lies in her bed and cries to
think we can't get on better in the world.
I'd help her, if I could, but I don't know
any thing to do."

It did not take long to reach the wet meadow, as Bessie called it. It lay only a stone's throw back of the house. It was called "wet," because a beautiful brook coursed through it, and moistened the ground so much as to render it unprofitable for cultivation. The watercresses had it all their own way. They grew wild over nearly the whole field, and extended down to the very edge of the brook, and leaned their beautiful bright leaves and graceful stems into the little stream, as it flowed over the pebbles.

Bessie led the farmer to a large, flat stone, where they could stand with dry feet and survey the scene. The sun was just setting; they could see the glow in the west through the grove of trees that skirted the outer edge of the field; the birds were just chirping their mournful October songs, as they flew about, seeking for a shelter for the coming night; the murmur of the brook added not a little to the serenity of the hour.

The farmer stooped, and reaching his hand among the wet earth where the cresses grew, plucked one, and tasted it.

"It is as fine as any I ever ate," said he, "and, as far as I see, your mother's meadow is full of just such ones. The frost and the cold winds have spoiled ours, but yours are protected by that hill back there, and are first-rate."

"Do you think we could get money for them?" cried Bessie, jumping up and down on the loose stone on which they stood, until it shook so as almost to make her lose her balance and fall into the water; "do you think people will *buy* them?"

"Certainly," said the farmer, giving his lips a final smack over the remnant of the cress, "certainly I do, and they are so clear from weeds it will be no trouble to gather them. What is your name, little girl?"

"Bessie, sir, and my mother's name is that too. Wouldn't you like to come in and see her for a moment, to tell her about the cresses?"

"Not to-day," said the farmer, shaking his head, and looking at the sinking sun; "it grows late, and I have a long journey to go, but I'll tell you what I *will* do. I go to market again the day after to-morrow, and I leave home at five o'clock in the morning, or thereabouts. Now, I'm sorry to hear of your mother's troubles, and I want to help her if I can. You tell her all I have said about the cresses bringing a good price, and see if she has any objections to your gathering a big basket full, and having it ready to send to market when I pass by. I can take one for you just as well as not, three or four times a week. Leave it just inside the gate, and I will get it, for it will be too early for you to be up."

"Yes, sir," said Bessie, her face perfectly radiant with smiles; "how good you are to take so much trouble — how good you are! I'll tell mother all about you, be sure of that."

"And now I must be off," said the farmer, stepping from the flat stone into the moist grass and picking his way as well as he could towards the house, and thence to the gate. Bessie followed him to the road, and watched him untie old Dobbin. The tears came in her eyes as she called out,

"Good-by, sir, good-by."

The farmer turned, half smiled to see how grateful the poor child looked, and said kindly,

"Good-by, Bessie."

CHAPTER III.

WATER-CRESSES.

BESSIE'S mother was both surprised and rejoiced to hear of the kindness of the farmer. It seemed to her a great stroke of good fortune. The little sum of money which she had saved in more prosperous days was almost exhausted, and it had been a bitter thought to her to know, that when this should be gone, they would have nothing. The little house in which they lived could be sold, it is true, but the widow had always looked upon it in the light of a *home*, and not as an article to be disposed of for support.

A ready consent was given that Bessie should try what she could do with the water-cresses. The little girl was delighted at the prospect, and already she saw herself the future possessor of a great deal of money.

Her mother wanted her to gather the cresses the night previous to the morning on which the farmer was expected, but in her enthusiasm, Bessie insisted that they would be far fresher and nicer when they reached market if she should do so at daybreak; and she promised faithfully to rise in sufficient time to accomplish the feat.

"But, my child," said her mother, "it will not be light enough for you to choose the best cresses, and the farmer may come before you get through, and of course we could not ask him to wait. No, gather them late in the afternoon, carefully select the poor ones, and the dead leaves and grasses that may be mingled with them, and the rest put in the oak pail and cover them with clean water. In the morning you can rise as early as you please, and fasten them up securely in the large basket, and be ready to give them to the farmer yourself, if you would like to do so when he passes."

Bessie acknowledged that this was wisest. Accordingly, towards the latter part of the day before the appointed morning, she provided herself with a basket and the garden scissors, to go down ·to the brook and begin her undertaking. Previous to doing so, however, she put her head in her mother's room and called out with a gay laugh, "good-by, mother, I am going to make a fortune for you yet, see if I don't!"

Her mother smiled, and when Bessie shut the door and jumped lightly down

the stairs, two at a time, she felt as though
her child's courage and hopefulness were
really infusing courage and hopefulness
into herself.

Singing at the top of her lungs, Bessie
set to work. Never had she felt as light-
hearted and happy. She tucked up her
calico dress a little way, into the strings
of her apron, in order to keep it out of the
wet, and drew off her shoes and stockings.
Then arming herself with the scissors, she
cut vigorously among the cresses; taking
care, however, to choose only those that
presented a fine appearance, for she was
determined that the first specimens the
farmer took with him, should be so fine as
to attract the attention of the buyers, and
thus induce them to come again. A
shrewd little business woman was Bessie !
She had her basket sitting on some stones

" She was clipping at the cresses, when she heard some one call her name." —
p. 45.

near her, and when she moved further up and down the brook, she was careful always to move that also. She was singing away as loudly and heartily as she could, and clipping at the cresses, when she heard some one call her name. She looked up, and there stood a boy about fourteen years old, named Martin, who lived on Nelly's father's farm. He looked as though he wanted very much to laugh at the odd figure which Bessie cut; her sun-bonnet hanging by its strings to her neck, her dress tucked up to the knees, a pair of shears in one hand, an enormous basket in the other, and both of her bare feet in the brook.

"Why, Bessie," said Martin, "what a noise you have been making! I called you four or five times *real loud*, and I whistled too, and yet you went on singing

'Old folks at home,' and 'Little drops of water,' as though your ears were not made to hear any voice but your own!"

"That's 'cause I'm *so* happy," said Bessie. "Why, Martin, I'm beginning to earn my own living, — think of *that*. Isn't it fun though?" and she splashed through the stream to have a nearer talk with her visitor.

"Earning your living!" repeated Martin; "well, I should call playing in the brook, as you seemed to be just now, any thing but that."

"Playing!" echoed Bessie, with some indignation, "I am a big girl of nine now, and I am not going to play any more; I am going to *work*. Don't you see these cresses?"

"Yes," said Martin, "but they're not good for much, are they?"

"Good!" laughed Bessie, capering about, quite unmindful of bare ankles, "Good! I shouldn't wonder *much* if they were. Why, Martin Wray, I'm to sell 'em, and get *money* for 'em — plenty of it — till my pockets are so full that they cannot hold any more — there!"

"Money!" said Martin, "you don't mean to say people buy cresses? What can they do with them?"

"Eat 'em," replied Bessie, promptly; "mother says rich folks buy them to make into salads, — mustard, pepper, salt, vinegar, and all that sort of thing, you know. Mother says they are just in their prime now."

Martin stooped and helped himself to a handful of the cresses. He did not seem to like their flavor, but made wry faces over them.

"Dear, dear," he said, "how they bite! They will take my tongue off."

"That's the beauty of 'em," said Bessie, coolly, "that's a proof that they are good. Mother says when they grow flat and insipid they don't bring a fair price."

"But isn't this late in the year for them?" asked her visitor.

"No," was the answer; "this is just the best of the fall crop, and they will last for a month or six weeks, and maybe all winter, if the season is mild. May is the great spring month for them, and October the one in the autumn. Mother told me she brushed the snow away from a little patch last Christmas, and there they were just as fresh and green as ever."

"And who are you going to sell them to?" asked Martin.

"A farmer," answered Bessie, "who

lives up in the nutting woods has promised to take them to market."

"Oh," said Martin, "that reminds me
of what I came for. Nelly knew I had
to pass by here to-day with a letter, and
she asked me to inquire if you would
go nutting with her and me to-morrow.
She wants to stop for another little girl
too, I believe."

"Dolly?" said Bessie.

"I don't know," replied Martin, "what
her name was. She said it was a girl
who had the fever and ague."

"That's Dolly!" cried Bessie, joyfully,
"Dolly has it *awful*. Just wait here a
minute while I run ask mother if she
can spare me."

She went skipping in the house, and
in a short time her bare feet were heard
skipping out again.

4

"Yes," she cried, triumphantly waving her sun-bonnet, "mother told me 'yes.'"

Martin now said he must go on and deliver his letter, and Bessie bade him good-by, and went back to her cresses. In a little while the basket was filled with the very finest the brook afforded, and she carried them in the house to place in water as her mother had directed.

The next morning, as the gray dawn came through the window of the room where she and her mother slept, Bessie awoke suddenly, and before she knew it she was sitting up in bed, drowsily rubbing her eyes. She had borne so well on her mind the appointment with the farmer, that she had awakened long before her usual time. She was a lazy girl generally, and liked very much to lie luxuriously in bed and *think about* getting up, without making an effort to do so. It was at least three hours earlier than it was her habit to rise, yet she did not stop to think of that, but bounded out and began her morning's ablution ; her mother having always striven to impress upon her the great fact that "cleanliness is next to godliness." It was but a short time when, leaving her mother, as she thought, soundly sleeping, Bessie crept noiselessly as possible down the stairs that led to the kitchen, and there carefully packed her cresses for market. When the basket was full, she wrapped hastily a shawl around her, to protect her from the chilly autumn air of the morning, and ran out to the gate to place it, ready for the farmer, when he should come along in his wagon. She stood on the cross bars of the, gate, and looked eagerly up and down the road, but she saw nothing as yet. The thought crossed her mind that Mr. Dart might already have passed the house, and finding no basket prepared for him, had driven on without it. But when she looked around, and saw how early it still appeared, how the gray was not gone from the sky, and the sun had not risen, nor the soft white morning mists yet rolled away from the mountains that lay to the left of the village, she was quite sure that she was not too late. She went back to the open door sill of the kitchen, which, being built in a small wing, fronted on the road, and sat down quietly on the sill. Presently she thought she heard the rattle of wheels, and the snapping of a whip. She ran to the gate, and looked in the direction from which it was to be expected the farmer would come, and there he was, seated on top of a load of turnips, trotting down the road as fast as old Dobbin could go, under the circumstances. He saw Bessie, and shook his whip over his head as a sort of salutation.

"Good morning," said Bessie, as soon as he was near enough to hear her voice.

"Good morning," replied the farmer, holding Dobbin up, so as to stop. "Well now, this looks something like! I guess you're most as smart as my Dolly, who got up and fixed breakfast before I started. What does mother say about the water-cresses, eh?"

"All right, sir," cried Bessie, joyfully,

lugging into view the basket, "and here they are, sir, all ready, — beauties, *every one* of 'em."

The farmer raised the cover, looked in, and whistled.

"Yes," said he, "this is the pick of the whole lot, I guess. But you haven't half big enough a basket. You must send more next time, for the frost may come and nip them a little, before you sell enough to be worth your while. Haven't you ever heard of making hay while the sun shines, Bessie?"

He took the basket and packed it nicely among the turnips, so that it would not jostle out with the movement of the wagon. As he did so, Bessie's mother, with a shawl hastily thrown around her, opened the window of her bedroom, and said sufficiently loud to be heard,

".Good morning, sir; I am afraid you are putting yourself to a great deal of trouble for us."

"Not at all, ma'am," said the farmer, quite surprised at her sudden apparition, and taking off his hat as he spoke; "on the contrary, it's quite a pleasure."

"I am very much obliged to you, I am sure," said the widow, "and Bessie is too. It is very kind of you to help us, poor people as we are, along in the world."

"Well, ma'am," said the farmer with a smile, "as far as that goes, I'm poor myself — poor enough, dear knows, and that's the very thing that sometimes makes me feel for other poor folks, particularly poor *sick* folks, for we 'most always have a spell of the nager at our house. But I must be off. I'll stop, ma'am, as I come back, about noon, to tell you what luck I have had with these ere cresses."

He was just going to drive on when Bessie said, "Oh, sir, I almost forgot. Is to-day Dolly's *well* day? Nelly and I thought of going nutting with her."

"Yes," . replied the farmer, "Doll is pretty smart to-day. Make no doubt she can go. Good morning, ma'am, good morning, Bessie;" and he touched up old Dobbin and trotted down the hill.

Bessie stood with the shawl over her head to watch the wagon as it seemed to grow less and less in size, and finally was hid by a curve of the road. Then she pulled to the gate to keep out stray cows from the little garden which her mother prized so much, and reëntered the kitchen.

She had a great many things to accomplish during the morning, because now that her mother was sick a number of household duties devolved upon her, with which she had nothing to do under ordinary circumstances. But, keep herself as busy as she could, the time still hung heavily. It seemed to her as if noon would never come. Her mother tried to hear her say her lessons in the intervals, when she had to sit up, but Bessie could not attend enough to repeat them well. She made many strange mistakes.

The top of every page in her spelling-book was decorated with a picture which illustrated whatever word stood at the head of the column. Thus, *chandelier*, *work-box*, *bedstead*, were each represented in a pretty engraving. I suppose this was done in order to excite the interest of the scholar. Bessie's thoughts to-day were so far away with her water-cresses, however, that she could think of nothing else. At the head of her column for the morning was the word *ladle,* and at its side was the picture of a stout servant girl, ladling out a plate of soup from a tureen. The shape of the ladle so much resembled a skimmer which Bessie had often seen in use in her mother's kitchen, that with her thoughts following the farmer in his wagon, she spelled and pronounced in this wise:

"L-a, skim, d-l-e, mer, *skimmer!*"

"My patience," said her mother, "what nonsense is that, Bessie, which you are saying?"

"L-a, skim, d-l-e, mer, skimmer," gravely repeated Bessie, quite unconscious of the droll mistake.

Her mother could not but laugh, but she asked her if such inattention was kind to herself when she was so ill as scarcely to be able to speak, much less to question over and over again a girl who did not care whether she learned or not.

"But I *do* care, mother," cried Bessie, coloring.

"Then why do you try me so? Take your book and study your spelling properly."

Bessie did so, and this time, mastering her inclination to think of other things, soon accomplished her task.

"It is not because you are a dull child," said her mother, "that you do not learn, but because you are a careless one. The least thing comes between you and your lessons. This morning, I suppose you are somewhat to be excused, but I cannot express to you how you weary me, day after day, by the same conduct."

These words filled Bessie with shame. She really loved her mother, and there were few things she would not have done to please her. She did not realize how simple thoughtlessness can pain and annoy those whom we would not purposely wound.

"Well, mother," said Bessie, casting down her eyes, "I *do* wish I was good. Maybe I am not big enough yet, am I, mother?"

Her mother smiled, saying, "You are plenty big enough, and plenty old enough too."

Bessie smiled too, and was happy to see that her mother was not as vexed with her as she thought. She went up to her and gave her a little shy kiss on her cheek.

"It is *such* hard work to be good," she said, "and it does *so* bother me to be thinkin' of it all the time. Wouldn't it be nice if we could be good without any trouble? When I am grown up I hope I'll be good, anyway."

"Oh Bessie," said her mother, seriously, "do not wait till then. While you are young is the time to break yourself of bad habits and slothful ways. If you wait until you become a woman, they will have fastened themselves upon you so that you cannot shake them off."

Just as Bessie's mother pronounced the last words, she heard a knock on one of the outer doors. Bessie heard it too, and ran down stairs to open it.

It was now nearly time to expect Mr. Dart, and her heart beat with delight at the anticipation of the news she was so soon to hear.

She opened the door, and saw, not the kind face of the farmer, but that of a small, ungainly boy, who lived in the next house. He was a sickly, spoiled child, and Bessie, never liking him much at the best of times, found him now rather an unwelcome visitor.

"Our folks wants to know if your mother'll lend us some sugar," he said, at the same time handing out a cracked tea-cup.

Bessie took the cup and invited the boy to go up and see her mother, while she brought the sugar. She had just filled the cup even full, when again she heard a knock. This time she felt sure it was the farmer, and indeed when she flew to the door, there he stood, smiling at her in the porch. One of his hands was extended towards her, and in its palm she saw three bright silver coins!

"Take them, Bessie," he said, "they are your own. Them cresses o' your'n were the best in market. I'm coming along to-morrow morning at the same time, and if you like, you can have another lot for me. Here's your basket, but it isn't half big enough, as I told you before."

Bessie stood holding the money in her hands, quite unable to utter a word. Her first thought was to dash up stairs and tell her mother, her next to run after the farmer and thank him. But he had already mounted into his seat and Dobbin, very glad to know that his nose

was turned homeward, had taken the
hint to start off at a pace that soon
placed his driver out of hearing.

"I am so sorry," said Bessie, gazing
after the wagon in much the same way
as she had done in the morning. " Mother
will say I forgot my politeness *that* time.
And he so kind too!"

She ran in the house again, and in a
moment was in her mother's room.

" Mother, mother," she cried, holding
out the coins, "you can have every
thing you want now! See, here's money,
plenty of it! I don't believe I ever saw
so much at once in all my life. How
many goodies you shall have to make
you well!"

Her mother was lying partially dressed
outside the bed-quilts, but she rose up
slowly to share Bessie's joy. Bessie put
the money in her hands and danced

around the room like a wild girl, utterly regardless of the fire-tongs that she whirled out of place, and a couple of chairs, which she laid very neatly flat on their sides in the middle of the floor. Then she flew at her mother and gave her two monstrous, *sounding* kisses on each cheek. Her mother gave them right straight back to her, and I can assure you Bessie wasn't at all sorry to have them returned.

"Why, Bessie," said the little boy, who had been a silent spectator all this time, "what is the matter with you? You act real crazy."

"I *am* crazy," said Bessie, good-humoredly, "just as crazy as can be. This is my water-cress money. Didn't you know I can earn money for mother? How much is there, mother?"

5

The widow spread out the three coins in her hand, and after a moment's pause, said,

"Here are two twenty-five cent pieces, and a ten cent piece; that makes just sixty cents."

Bessie sat perfectly still, and when her mother looked at her, attracted by an unusual sound, she had her apron up to her eyes, crying as peacefully as possible.

"Why, my foolish little girl," said her mother, "I can't have any tears shed in this way. Jump up like a good child and get Nathan his sugar."

"I couldn't help it," sobbed Bessie, "I didn't know I was agoin' to till I did."

"What are you thinking of doing with it all?" asked Nathan, eyeing the money with some curiosity.

"Save it," answered Bessie, promptly, "till mother gets ready to use it." She went to a table standing at the head of the bed, and from its drawer she took out a large-sized Madeira nut, that had been given to her by her uncle the previous Christmas. The two halves were joined together by a steel hinge, and when a small spring was touched on the opposite side, they opened. Bessie touched it now, and advancing to her mother, said,

"Let's keep the money in this nut, mother, for a purse, until you want to spend it."

Her mother dropped the silver in the open shell, and Bessie closed it and replaced it in the drawer. Then she and Nathan went down to get the sugar.

CHAPTER IV.

HUNGRY FISHES.

It was about two o'clock when Bessie, basket in hand, started to go on the nutting excursion which Nelly and Martin had planned for that day.

She scarcely liked to be absent long, for she knew her mother was not quite as well as usual, and then, too, the water-cresses were to be gathered and prepared for the next day's market. At all events she made up her mind to get home early, long before the sun should set.

It was but a short walk of a half mile to Nelly's home; Martin and Nelly were ready, so that no time was consumed in waiting.

It was even a more beautiful day than the one on which the previous nutting had taken place. The woods were brighter colored than ever, and the golden autumn mist seemed to cover every thing with beauty. It hung in wreaths around the tops of the high trees, and swayed softly back and forth when the breeze stirred it. The boats on the river could scarcely be discerned through it, and the opposite shores were entirely hidden.

"This is Dolly's *well* day," said Bessie, "I asked her father and he told me so."

"Martin says you are going to sell him some water-cresses," said Nelly; "at least, I suppose he was the one; did you?"

"Yes," said Bessie; "that is, he sold them *for* me, which is the same thing you know. He brought me three *big* pieces of money for them at noon, and I put 'em in a nut-shell and shut 'em up."

"A nut-shell?" repeated Martin, "that is a funny bank, I think."

"It's a safe one," said Bessie, "and it will not break and keep the money like some of those I have heard of in town. Just look at those bitter-sweets, Nell, aren't they bright?"

"I mean to get some," cried Nelly, as she paused to admire the red sprays of the berries that grew at the side of the short-cut path they were pursuing. "I will take them home to mother to put in her winter bouquets of dried grasses, that stand on the parlor mantle-shelf.

They will enliven them and make them much handsomer."

"Why not wait till we return?" said Martin; "you will have all the trouble of carrying them to the woods and back again, and perhaps lose them by the way."

"I know too much for that," said Nelly, laughing; "we may not come back by this road, and then I should not get them at all. Last week I lost some in the same way: I went out walking with Miss Milly over the mountains, and we came to some beauties near Mulligan's little shanty. We thought to save ourselves trouble by leaving them till we returned. Something or other tempted us to strike into another path when we came back, so that our bitter-sweets are on the top of the mountain yet."

"No," said Bessie, "I don't think they
are. Did they grow over a big rock,
and were there plenty of sumach bushes
between them and the path?"

"Yes," said ·Nelly, beginning to pull
down the rich clusters of the bitter-
sweets, and breaking them off, one by
one.

"Well," said Bessie, making a deep,
mock courtesy, "I have the pleasure of
having those berries in my own bedroom at this blessed minute. I went to
Mulligan's on an errand of mother's, a
few days ago, and I brought them down
the mountain with me."

"Her loss was your gain, wasn't it?"
said Martin, as he aided Nelly to gather
the berries.

"I'll help too," said Bessie, "for I'm
in a *dreadful* hurry to get back, Nelly.

I have all my cresses to pick for market," and she too broke off the bunches and laid them carefully in Nelly's basket.

"What!" said Nelly, "*more* cresses, Bessie?"

"Yes," said Bessie, giving a joyful hop, and, as her mother called it, cutting a caper; "and that isn't all, for Dolly's father wants lots and lots *and* lots more of 'em! Come, I guess you have plenty now, let's go on."

Nelly consented to do so, but first Martin took out of his pocket a handful of tangled twine, and with a piece of it tied the bitter-sweet berries together by the stems, and suspended them in a bunch from her apron strings, so that her basket might be ready for the nuts.

Martin was a farm boy who worked at Nelly's father's place. He was a good, steady lad, and the two girls liked very much to have his company in their excursions. It was not often, however, that he could be spared, and the present occasion was, therefore, quite a holiday in his estimation.

When the children reached the little house near the wood, they were surprised to see Dolly standing in the gateway quite equipped for the ramble. She had a large basket on her arm, and a long hickory stick in her hands. Nelly introduced Martin, who stood a little aloof when the girls first met, and then Dolly asked them if they would not all come in and rest, but the children thought that it was best not to do so. Hearing voices, the farmer came to the door of the farm house to see them off. He looked pleased to find Dolly with the little girls.

" Martin told the girls that if they would place themselves with him on an old
trunk of a tree, they would probably find it to be a better position from which to
throw their lines." — p. 93.

"That's right," he said, "I'm glad to have my Dolly tramping about like other folks' children. It will do her good. But don't stay late: the damp of the evening is very unwholesome for the nager."

"Oh, we are coming back long before night, sir," said Bessie, cheerfully, "'cause I've got all my cresses to pick for to-morrow. ·Mother and I are *so* much obliged to you, I can't really *tell* how much!"

"Quite welcome, quite welcome," said Mr. Dart; "I'll be on the look-out for another basket to-morrow then."

As the four children walked briskly along the path through the woods, Nelly looked with some curiosity at Dolly's stick. She could not imagine for what purpose it was intended. It was not very stout, nor apparently very heavy;

at the upper end it was a little curved. Dolly seemed to use it for a staff, and several times helped herself over some rough and stony places with it. When the walking was good she carried it carelessly over her shoulder, with her basket swinging at the crooked end.

A short time brought the party to the place where they had found so many nuts only a day or two before. *Much to their surprise and mortification the trees which were lately so loaded, were now perfectly bare. Some one had evidently been there during the time that intervened, and had carried away the prize. There were several large piles of the outer shells scattered about on the ground, but that was all.

"What shall we do," asked Bessie, mournfully; "I don't think we can find another such spot as this was in the whole woods. This clump of trees was as full as it could be only the day before yesterday."

Dolly took her stick and poked among the branches to see if any remained. She found about half a dozen, which she knocked down and put in her basket.

"Now I know," said Nelly, "what Dolly brought that pole for,— to knock down the nuts."

"Yes," said Dolly, surveying the stick in question with some pride, "it is splendid for that. I call it my cherry-tree hook, and I use it in cherry time to pull the branches towards me. But come, we must push on and seek our fortunes. Haven't an *idee* of goin' home without my basket full."

"I give up, for one," said Bessie, despondently, "I don't think we can find a thick place again."

"Never mind, Bessie," said Martin, with good-nature, "we'll find a *thin* one then. We'll do the best we can, you may be sure. Come, girls, I'll lead the way. Let us follow this little foot-path and see where it will take us."

He spoke in an encouraging tone, and suiting the action to the word, walked on ahead. The girls followed him in silence. The underbrush through which the path led was very thick and high, and for a short distance nothing could be discerned on either side. The thorns caught into the clothing of the little party, and they found this by no means an added pleasure. It was not long, however, before the track broadened into a wide, open space, something similar to the one they had just quitted, dotted here and there with trees, but, as fortune would have it, none of them were nut trees. They were on the point of penetrating still further towards the heart of the wood, when a loud rustling among the dead branches and dried leaves of the path made the children turn to discover what was the matter.

A joyful barking followed, and a rough-looking dog bounded out, and began prancing about and leaping upon Dolly.

" Oh, it's only our old Tiger," she exclaimed; "down, Tige, down, sir!"

But Tiger was so delighted at having succeeded in finding his young mistress, that he did not cease indulging in his various uncouth gambols, until Dolly, stamping her foot and assuming an air of great severity, bade him *be quiet,* or she would send him immediately home. Tiger seemed to understand the threat, for he stopped barking and instantly darted several hundred feet in advance of the party.

"He does that so that I cannot make him go back," cried Dolly, laughing at the sagacity of her favorite; "I never tell him I will send him home, but that he runs ahead so as to make it impossible for me to do as I say."

They continued their wanderings for some distance further, but with very poor success.

"I'll tell you what we can do," said Martin, with a laugh, as exclamations of vexation and disappointment were heard from the girls; "let's turn our nutting into a fishing excursion. Wouldn't it be nice if we should each go home with a string of fish?"

"Fish!" cried Nelly, "what *do* you mean, Martin?"

"I never heard of anybody catchin' fish in the woods!" said Dolly. "There isn't a drop of water nearer than the pond the other side of Morrison's hill."

"Well," said Martin, "I know there is not, but that is not so very far off. I was just thinking of the shortest way to get there."

"I know every inch of the country," said Dolly, firmly, "and I'm *sure* Morrison's pond is at least a good two mile from here."

"Oh, we can't walk *that*, Martin," cried Bessie; "we should all be tired, and get home after dark besides."

"Now," said Martin, smiling, "I do not wish to contradict anybody, but I am acquainted with a path, a rather rough one to be sure, that will bring us, in about twenty minutes, to the edge of the pond. You know it is not as far away as people think, the crooked, winding road making it appear a long way off, when in reality it lies in a straight line only about half a mile from the village."

"But if we conclude to go, we can't *fish*," said Dolly.

"Why not?" quietly asked Martin.

"We haven't a line or a hook among us," put forth Nelly, "at least I am sure *I* haven't."

"Well *I* have," replied Martin, "provided you will not despise bent pins for hooks, pieces of the twine that is left

of that I tied your bitter-sweet berries
with for lines, a hickory stick like Dolly's
for a rod, and earth worms for bait.
There now, haven't I furnished the
whole party with tackle? Come, don't
let us go home without having *something*
to take with us."

Dolly sat down on the stump of a
tree and began to laugh.   .

"The idee," she said, "of going nutting and bringing home *fish*. Well, I'm
willing, for one, if it's only to find out
the path. I thought I knew all the
ins and outs around here."

"And I'd like to go too," said Nelly.

"I should *like* to go well enough,"
added Bessie, "if it wasn't that I feel
sure the extra walk will just bring me
home too late for my cresses. Mother
is sick, too, and she cannot be left alone

very long; and Dolly, you know your father said you must not stay out late."

"Yes," said Dolly, "I know he did, and I don't mean to disobey, but it can't be very late *yet*; I should think not more than half past three."

Martin looked up at the sun and then down to the shadows on the ground.

"No," said he, "it is not more than half past three. I am in the habit of telling time by the sun, and I know it is not later than that. Come, Bessie, three to one is the way the case stands. I guess you will be home time enough."

Bessie stood irresolute. She wished to go fishing, and she wished to return home. It was hard to choose. At last she said,

"It will be four at least when I get back. I must go."

"Then you break up the party," said Nelly, in a dissatisfied tone.

"And you spoil the pleasure," added Dolly, leaning on her stick and looking at Bessie.

"And you send us all home with empty baskets when we might each have a string of fish," continued Martin. "*Do* stay!"

The children surrounded Bessie, and tried to persuade her. At length she ceased to resist. She endeavored to assure herself that she was acting right, but she felt uneasy as she did so, and the picture of her mother, lying so long alone in her sick room, rose up to her mind. Still the temptation was before her, and she yielded to it. The truth was, that Bessie had great confidence in Martin, and when he said that he thought there was plenty of time, she reasoned with herself that he was a great deal older than she was, and probably knew best; so she consented to join the fishing party. The moment she said "yes," Martin exclaimed,

"This way then; follow me, all of you, and we will soon reach the short-cut track. It is about here somewhere. Let us hurry so as to lose no time."

The path was speedily found as he had said, and the children walked as rapidly after him as the rough stones which lay in the way, and the projecting branches of blackberry bushes would permit.

When they reached the pond, Martin took out the pocket knife which he usually carried about him, and cut down four slender young trees which he found growing between the pond and the public wagon-road at its side. He gave these to Nelly and asked her if she would tie the strings securely fast to the smallest ends, while he and Bessie overturned stones in search of worms, and Dolly bent the points of the pins so as to resemble hooks.

"Why will not my staff do for a pole?" asked Dolly, as she hammered at the pins with a large pebble; "you said it would, Martin."

"That was before I saw these little trees," replied Martin. "The moment I came upon them, growing here in a group among the bushes, I knew they were just the things I wanted. They are thin and tapering, and your stick is not."

"What difference does that make?"

said Dolly; "a pole is only for the purpose of casting the line out a good distance into the water, isn't it?"

"That is one use for it," said Martin, "but not all. If a pole is properly proportioned, that is, if it is the right size at the handle, and tapers gradually to the point, the fisherman can feel the least nibble, and know the exact moment when to draw up the line. If he could not feel the movement, the fish might, in the struggles occasioned by his pain, carry off bait and hook too."

"In our case that wouldn't be a great loss," laughed Dolly, and she held up the pins, neatly bent into shape.

"Martin," said Bessie, in a low voice, as she stooped to raise a stone at his side, "I guess I don't care to fish, after all."

Martin saw something was amiss. Instead of giving utterance to a rude exclamation, or calling the attention of the others, he said in a kind tone,

"Why, Bessie, what is the matter now? Don't you feel right?

Bessie shook her head. Martin saw there were tears in her eyes.

"I am sorry I coaxed you," he said. "I feel now as if I had not behaved as I ought."

"I never *did* like to go fishing," said Bessie; "it *hurts* me to see the poor little things pant and flounder when they are brought up. The moment I heard you speak of their struggling with the pain, I was sorrier than ever that I had come, and that made me think of mother, staying home alone with *her* pain. I do believe I ought to go back at once."

"But you cannot find the way," said Martin; "you have never been here before."

"That is true," said Bessie, sighing. "Well, I do not wish to be a spoil-pleasure. Don't mind me, then, but you and the others begin your fishing, and if I see a wagon come by on the road that is going our way, I can jump in. I need not stop your sport if I do that."

Martin looked perplexed.

"I hardly like you to try it," he said, "and yet I do not wish you to stay against your will."

"Well," said Bessie, "I don't like to act *mean*, Martin. Go on fishing for a little while, at all events. I can wait half an hour or so, I suppose."

Nelly now called to Martin that the lines were ready, for Dolly had just finished tying on the last pin. He gathered up the bait he had found beneath the stones, and went towards the two other girls. He thought, on consideration, that he might fish for a short time, while waiting to see if a wagon approached on the road. If none did so within the allotted half hour, he made up his mind to go home. He blamed himself now for having changed the destination of the party.

"Here's my line," cried Dolly, holding it out at the end of her pole, "and now all that I and the fishes wait for is a worm."

Martin fastened one on Dolly's pin, one on Nelly's likewise, and one on the line he intended for himself.

"Come, Bessie,' said Nelly, as she flung her line into the water, "come try *your* luck."

"Bessie does not care about fishing," said Martin kindly, "do not press her if she does not wish it."

The pond was well stocked with a variety of small fishes, many of which were considered good eating by the farmers in the neighborhood. As scarcely any one ever took the trouble, however, to go after them, they were hardly acquainted with hooks or lines, and they were, consequently, all the more easily caught. Martin said he had never seen such hungry fishes before. They snapped at the bait the moment it was lowered to them, oftentimes carrying it entirely off, hook and all.

Once, and the children could scarcely believe it when they saw it, a fish called a bull-head leaped at least an inch above the water and tried to swallow the end of Dolly's line, which she was in the act of raising, to replace the pin and worm which some of his greedy kindred had just taken away.

Martin told the girls that if they would place themselves. with him on an old trunk of a tree that apparently had fallen years before into the edge of the pond, they would probably find it to be a better position from which to throw their lines than the shore on which they had stood at first. "For," said he, "the larger fish do not like to venture into such shallow water." The trunk, however, was covered with moist moss, which made it very slippery, and Nelly came so near losing her balance and falling in, as she walked up it, that she concluded to remain where she was. Martin and Dolly did not meet with the

same difficulty, however, and very soon
they discovered that the nibbles were
far more frequent than before. Martin
kept a twig on which he slipped the
fish as soon as caught, and then hung
it on a branch of the moss-covered trunk.
Bessie had begun to look on the pro-
ceedings with interest, feeling almost as
sorry as her companions as a ravenous
bull-head occasionally carried off the
hooks, when she heard a noise on the
road as of wheels. She ran to the
bushes which divided it from the pond,
and putting her little face through, saw
that the miller who lived in the village
was passing with three or four large
sacks of meal in a wagon drawn by a
pair of horses. He was going the wrong
way, but the thought occurred to her
to stop him and ask how long it would

be before he should return, and if he should do so by the same road. The miller was a stout, good-natured looking man, with an old hat and coat as white as his meal bags. · He seemed astonished enough at seeing Bessie's head pop so suddenly out of the bushes in that lonely place.

"Why, Bessie," said he, laughing, "if I hadn't been as bold as a lion, perhaps I might have mistaken you for a mermaid that had just sprung out of the pond to have a little private conversation with me. Yes, I shall come back by this road. I have got to deliver my meal at the first house on the left, and then I turn towards home again. Is that your party that I catch a glimpse of on the pond?"

"Yes," said Bessie, "they're fishing.

You wouldn't mind giving us a ride as far as you go, Mr. Watson, would you?"

Mr. Watson laughed, and said no he wouldn't, and telling her he should return in fifteen minutes, he drove on. Bessie hurried back to the children and related her news. She was careful not to be so selfish as to ask them to leave the pond to go with her, but she told them for their own benefit that the miller was willing to take the whole party. Enticing as the fishing was, the two girls were now far too tired to desire to walk home when they could ride very nearly all the way. Martin for his part would have liked to remain longer, but he saw that it would be ungenerous to refuse to accompany them, even if it had been early enough to do so, which it was not, for already the day was on the wane. So it was decided to leave the pond.

Martin put Dolly's share of the fishes on a separate twig, and very proud she was of them. She said she should fry them for her father's breakfast the next morning, before he started for market. The fishing poles were left lying near the old tree.

When the miller drove up to the place where Bessie had hailed him, he found the children awaiting him. Dolly and Martin, fish in hand, Nelly carrying her bitter-sweet berries, and Bessie with an empty basket, but a light heart at the thought that now she should reach home in good season to gather the cresses.

7

CHAPTER V.

LOST.

"I can't find it," said Bessie, about a month after the fishing party. "I have hunted high and low. I cannot find it anywhere."

Her mother, whose health was now greatly improving, was sitting in the kitchen by the blazing fire, for the weather was gradually growing colder, and the logs were piled up a little higher on the hearth, day by day. She was busy finishing quilting a white counterpane for a neighbor who employed her frequently to sew for her family. It was full of quaint devices, stars and diamonds forming the border, while in the centre was a wonderful little lamb in the act of performing some very frisky gambols.

. " Cannot find what ? " demanded Bessie's mother.

"My Madeira nut!" exclaimed Bessie, in a tone of despair. "Oh, what shall I do? what shall I do?"

Her mother stopped quilting and turned to look at her.

"Where did you put it last?" she asked. "Surely, Bessie, you ought to remember that."

"I have never put it in but one spot," replied Bessie; "I left it in the drawer • of my little table. When you grew better, and the table wasn't needed any more in your bedroom for you to stand your medicines on, I got Nathan to help me take it up stairs in the garret, just as you bade me, that day last week when he was here spending the afternoon. I thought I would still keep the nut there, for I had grown used to the place, and I liked to go to the drawer and pull it out to look at it sometimes. Oh dear, oh dear!" and Bessie burst into tears.

"Perhaps you haven't searched well," said her mother; "come, I'll go up stairs with you. I shouldn't wonder if it had got caught in the top of the drawer. I have heard of such things. I lost a handkerchief that way myself once."

"But," sobbed Bessie, "it couldn't get caught like that without being broken, because it was so thin shelled, and then I should have seen some of the pieces; or the money would have fallen back into the drawer, and I would have found *that.*"

"How much was in it?" asked her mother. "There could not have been a great deal more than the very first silver Mr. Dart brought you for the cresses, for the rest we have spent from time to time as fast as it was received. I was sorry enough to do it too." .

"I wasn't," said Bessie, brightening up a little through her tears, "I was glad and thankful, mother, to have it to spend. If it had not been for the cresses, what would have become of us all the while you were so sick?"

"God always provides for the poor and needy," said her mother gravely, "and I am certain that He who knows even when sparrows fall would not let us suffer. If this help had not sprung up for us through Mr. Dart, something else would have presented itself. Come, now, let us go to the garret and look for the money."

Bessie darted ahead of her mother as they went up the stairs, with a bound and a spring that brought her to the head of the flight when her mother was on the second step. She was young and agile, and besides she was greatly excited and in haste to begin the search. She did not gain any thing by her speed, however, for she had to wait at the landing until her mother had toiled slowly up.

"Now let us look at the drawer," said her mother, when, after pausing a moment to breathe, she moved towards the table. It was a poor little shaky thing, and of a very dilapidated appearance. It was not to be wondered at that as soon as her recovery made its presence unnecessary in her room, she had banished it to the garret whence it had been brought.

"You see there is no trace of it," said Bessie, mournfully, as she watched her mother remove the articles the drawer contained one by one.

No, it was not there indeed.

Bessie pulled out the drawer, and even took the trouble to examine the aperture which contained it, but all was in vain.

"It is certainly very strange," said her mother. "I do not see how, if it were really in this drawer, it could have got out without help."

"Nor I either," added Bessie, half laughing at the idea of a nut walking

off of itself. "Oh, if I could only find
it! I do not mind the nut so much,
although dear uncle James gave it to
me last Christmas, as I do the money,
for you know, mother, I asked you if
I might not keep it forever, that is as
long as I lived, to remember Mr. Dart's
kindness by, and to show, when I grew
up, as my first earnings. Oh, I was so
proud of those three pieces of silver!"

"What were they?" asked her mother,
looking over the contents of the drawer
again.

"*Don't you remember?*" exclaimed Bessie, in a tone of great surprise, as though
it were really remarkable to have forgotten. "Don't you remember? There
were two twenty-five cent pieces and a
ten cent piece!" and Bessie broke into
fresh weeping again.

"Don't cry about it, Bessie," said her mother, "you know crying cannot bring them back."

"I wouldn't care," said the little girl, "if it had been *yesterday's* money, but it was the first, *the very first* I ever earned of myself, and I meant to save it always!"

"I think I can tell you exactly how it happened, my child. Just look at the untidy appearance of your drawer. There are scraps in it of a great many things that ought not to be there. Here is a broken slate, your worn-out work-basket, your summer sun-bonnet, empty bottles, spools of cotton, and last but not least, about a quart of hickory nuts, — a nice array, I am sure."

Bessie hung her head. She was ashamed to have her disorderly ways remarked. A want of neatness was her greatest fault.

"I was just going to clear it up to-morrow," she murmured, twitching rather uneasily at her apron strings.

"Oh, my little girl, that 'just going' of yours is one of the saddest things I can hear you say. You are always '*just going*,' and yet the time seldom comes that you do as you intend. You are full of good intentions that you are either too lazy or too thoughtless ever to fulfil. If I did not watch over you very sharply, every thing you have would be like this miserable looking drawer, a complete mass of disorder."

"Oh, I hope not!" cried Bessie, quite appalled at the news.

"Now," continued her mother, "I can trace the losing of your money back to your want of neatness. In all probability, when you came to this drawer some time to get a few of your hickory nuts, you have caught up the Madeira among the others, carried it down stairs, and left the whole pile lying as you often do, somewhere around the garden till you feel in the humor for cracking them. I want to know, in the first place, why your hickory nuts were ever put in this drawer among your books and spools of cotton."

Bessie had been growing warmer and warmer while her mother was speaking, until it seemed to her as though the tips of her ears were on fire. Conviction forced itself upon her mind that her Madeira nut must have gone in the way her mother described, for she remembered distinctly having often taken two

or three handfuls of nuts and carried
them in her apron down to the garden,
leaving them lying carelessly about her
favorite resorts, under the old apple-tree
for instance, or on the big flat stone by
the brook. She had many just such
idle, unsystematic ways of managing.
She felt she was in the wrong, so she
scarcely knew how to defend herself.

"I don't know why I put the nuts
there, mother," she said, "unless it was
to get them out of the way. They are
those that are left of the basket full I
found in the woods by Mr. Dart's farm,
one day when Nelly and I went there
together."

"When *will* you learn neatness, Bessie ?"

"I don't know," sobbed Bessie, "never,
I 'spect. Seems to me I grow worse

and worse. I don't believe I shall be half as good when I am ten as I am now when I'm only nine. I wish I had never gone nutting, and then this would not have happened."

"No," said her mother, smiling, "it never would, for then in all probability you would not have met and become friendly with our good Mr. Dart. Don't make rash wishes, my little Bess, because you are vexed."

"Oh, now I know," cried Bessie, as if struck with a sudden idea, "I put the nuts in that drawer, mother, for *safety*. Before that they were lying spread out to dry on the floor, over by that barrel. I remember thinking that they were thinning out pretty fast, and that the rats must have carried some away. I thought that if I put them in the drawer they would last until I used them up."

"Well," said her mother, "that betters the case a little; but still I must insist that you could have found many more appropriate places. If you had put them in the barrel it would have been far better than among your spools, and I do not know but that it would have been quite as safe."

Bessie's mother went up to the barrel in question, as she spoke, and scarcely knowing what she was doing, shoved it a little with her foot. It was empty, and yielded easily. This change in its position brought to view the space between it and the wall, and there, what did Bessie and her mother see but a nice little pile of hickory nut-shells!

Bessie uttered an exclamation and

sprang forward. She took up two or three, and found that a hole had been neatly nibbled in each and the meat subtracted.

"I told you so," she said sorrowfully, letting the shells drop slowly back to the pile; "now I know why my nuts disappeared so fast. I thought at first that Nathan must have helped himself to a few, when he has been here. He often runs up stairs to get something or other to play with, when he stays the whole afternoon, and I guessed the nuts had tempted him. Poor Nathan! I ought to have known better."

Bessie's mother stooped and examined every shell in the pile.

"Perhaps," said she, "master rat has carried off the Madeira too."

"Oh, I hope so," cried the little girl;

"do you see any of the pieces of it, mother? He could not harm the money you know, and that is what I care most about getting back."

"It is not here," said her mother, rising, "but perhaps we shall hear something of it yet. I want you to put on your sun-bonnet and look carefully about the garden. Take an hour, or two hours if necessary, but do it thoroughly. I must go down stairs now to my sewing."

Bessie found it very tedious, sad work searching for her lost treasure that afternoon. She went to each of her favorite haunts, and examined them with great minuteness, but no trace of the nut was to be discovered. One thing seemed to her as very strange, however, and that was, that of all the small supplies of nuts which she had lately carried down to the garden, and of which she did not remember even to have cracked a single one, not so much as a fragment of a shell was now to be found. Only the day before she had left a little strawberry basket half filled, on the big stone by the brook, to which the reader remembers she once led Mr. Dart to survey the cresses. She had meant to sit there and crack and pick them out at once, at her leisure, but something attracting her attention as usual, she did not do so, but deserted both basket and nuts. The basket was there still, but to her surprise, it was quite empty. It lay on its side near where she had left it. No mark of any one having been there was to be seen in the muddy grass.

Bessie took up the basket and gazed

at it in silent astonishment. What could
it mean? Who would help themselves
to her nuts in this way? and why was
the basket not carried off also? She
was still sitting on the stone thinking
the whole singular affair over, when she
heard Nathan call to her from the next
house, where he lived. She looked up,
and there he was leaning over the
fence. She had just been thinking of
him, and it made her feel unpleasantly
to see him.

"Bess," cried he, "what do you think?
father is going to give me a ride to
town to-morrow."

Bessie scarcely heard him as she rose,
and holding up her empty basket, said
reproachfully, —

"Oh, Nathan, how could you climb
over the fence and take my nuts?"

"Nuts!" echoed Nathan, "what nuts? I don't know any thing about your nuts."

"Somebody does," said Bessie, "for this basket was half full yesterday, and now it is empty. I left it here on the stone all night."

"I never saw it," said Nathan; "that's mighty pretty of you to accuse a fellow of stealing. You had better be a little careful."

"I didn't say you *stole*, Nathan, I only —"

"Who cares for your old nuts?" interrupted Nathan, "they're not worth the carrying off. Next thing you'll be saying I meddle with your cresses."

"No," said Bessie, a little sadly, "I shouldn't say that. There are only two or three baskets-full of nice ones left, and by next week Mr. Dart will have taken them all to market. I don't *care* about my nuts, Nathan, it isn't that, but I should like to know who took them."

" Well, *I* didn't, anyhow," said Nathan, "and since you are so cross about it, I shan't stay to talk to you."

He clambered down from the fence and walked away whistling, with his hands in his pockets.

Some way, Bessie felt a presentiment that Nathan knew more than he said about the nuts. She concluded to go in and ask her mother if it could possibly be that he had taken the missing money.

Her mother listened in silence to all she had to utter on the subject. Bessie told her that Nathan was aware, and had been aware from the beginning, where the Madeira nut was kept. She said he was present when she first put it in the drawer, which was indeed true, as the reader knows, and that often since, they had looked at it together.

"My dear," said her mother, when Bessie concluded, "I do not see that you have any thing more than *conjecture* on which to found your suspicions. It is very wrong to act on conjecture only."

"But everybody thinks Nat is a bad boy," said Bessie eagerly; "the neighbors say he will do almost any thing. Only last Sunday he pinned the minister's coat tails to the shade of the church window, as he stood talking to Deacon Danbury, after meeting was over. When the minister went to walk off, down came the shade on his head and smashed his new hat. *I* think that a boy who will do that would take things that do not belong to him."

"Perhaps he might," said her mother quietly.

"Well, shall I ask him about it," demanded Bessie.

"My dear child," said her mother gravely, "your ideas of justice are one-sided. The world would not thrive if every one acted on the principles you seem to advocate. Many an honest man might be imprisoned as a thief if people should take mere *conjecture* for proof of guilt, while at the same time, many a thief would pass for an honest man. In law, all persons are supposed innocent, until they are *proved* guilty. You did not *see* Nathan take any thing belonging to you, nor do you know any one who did. It would be the height of cruelty then, to accuse him without absolute proof."

"Yes," said Bessie, "but suppose he *did* take the nut after all."

"Then," said her mother, "we can only leave the case to that Judge who doeth all things well. It is better for us to suppose him innocent even while he may be guilty, than to suppose him guilty when he is innocent."

"I wish I *knew*," said Bessie, as she took up her shears and basket to go out to get the cresses for the next day's market.

"The cold weather will soon put a stop to the cresses, I am afraid," remarked her mother, after a pause.

"Yes," said Bessie, "Mr. Dart says

they are getting poor now; they do not grow fast after cutting, any more, on account of the frost."

"Never mind," said her mother cheerfully, "in the spring, which after all is not so *very* far off, they will become fine again, and then you can begin to sell as fast as ever. If I am well then, as I hope and trust I shall be, we must not touch a penny of your money, Bessie. It shall all be saved to send you regularly to Miss Milly's school, and buy books for you to learn out of, and perhaps, who knows, there will be something left to put in the bank besides. This fall the cresses have fed our poor, suffering bodies, but next spring, if nothing happens, they shall feed my Bessie's mind."

"School!" cried Bessie, dropping both the basket and the scissors in her delight, "shall I *really* go to school? And all through the water-cresses? Why, we never thought our dear little brook would make us so rich, did we, mother?"

CHAPTER VI.

THE NEST.

ONE clear and cold morning in winter, as Bessie was passing along the road that led by Nelly's home, she heard Martin call her from the barn where he was at work. He saw her passing and beckoned to her to come to him. Bessie had the singular habit which most children possess of stopping to ask why she was summoned, when at the same time she fully intended to answer the call in person. So she stood still, and in a loud voice cried,

"Mar-TIN, what *is* it? What do you want of me?"

"Come and see!" replied Martin, "I've something nice to show you!" and then he resumed his place at the hay-cutting machine, at which he had been busy when he espied her. He was mincing the hay for the cattle to eat.

Bessie still stood irresolute. She meant to come, but she desired her curiosity to be gratified before she did so.

"Mar-TIN?"

"Well?"

"Can't you tell me *now* what it is?"

"No," replied Martin, going on with his hay chopping; "I guess you will have to come and see for yourself. It almost splits my throat to be calling out to you so."

"I think you might tell me," said Bessie, opening the gate and walking towards him; "you could have done it in half the time that you have been talking about it. Mercy! have you cut all that pile of hay this morning?"

"Yes," said Martin; "it's for the horses. I sprinkle a little water on it, and they like it a great deal better than when it is dry and uncut. It's healthier for them too."

"I am glad I don't live on it," said Bessie. "I should be like the horse that his master fed on shavings,—just as I got used to it I should die."

"Very likely," said Martin, laughing. "Come, and I'll show you what I spoke about." Bessie followed him as he led the way across the yard to the part of the barn where the large folding-doors were situated. They were wide open, and the clear winter sunshine streamed on the floor. An old wagon and a lad-

" A couple of white sheep came running eagerly up to Martin's outstretched
hand."—p 125.

der were placed across this opening, so that no one could come in or go out without climbing over.

" What is this for? " asked Bessie. " This wagon don't belong here, Martin. I never saw it here before."

" That's to keep the cows out," said Martin, smiling. " We have treasures in this part of the barn that it would not do for the cattle to get at. Here Nanny, here Jinny!"

A pattering of little hoofs was heard on the wooden floor, and a couple of white sheep came running eagerly up to Martin's outstretched hand. They rubbed themselves against it, and showed in various other ways how glad they were to see him.

" Aren't they pretty? " said Bessie admiringly. " Come here, Nanny."

But Nanny would not touch Bessie's hand, and backed up the barn, shaking her head at the sight of it, and kicking her delicate little heels in the air.

"They don't know you yet," said Martin, "but they are very tame, and would soon become acquainted if you were with them every day as I am. We have had them two weeks, and already they let me play with them. They are cossets."

"*Cossets*, Martin?"

"Yes; that means the pets of the flock. The cosset lamb means the pet lamb."

"Pet is a prettier word than cosset," said Bessie; "I should never call them that. I do wish mother had two such nice sheep. But why do you keep them shut up here?"

"You haven't seen all yet," said Martin, smiling; "just creep through this place and round by these wheels, and we will go in and find out why the cows are kept out and the sheep kept in."

Martin helped Bessie through the obstructions, and led her to the back of the barn where, nestled in a heap of clean hay that was piled against the opposite folding doors, she saw a little bundle of something white, in which she could just detect two small, glittering eyes.

"It's a lamb," cried Bessie, skipping about as if she were one herself.

"Two of 'em," said Martin. "Only look here!" and he pulled apart the loose whisps of hay, and there lay revealed two of the fattest, whitest, and

prettiest lambs that ever were seen.
They did not seem to like being admired,
but gave utterance to a little sharp cry
very much like a baby's. Hearing it,
one of the sheep trotted up, and pushing
between them and Martin, quietly began
to lick them.

"That's their mother," said Martin.
"They are twins, and only two days old.
The other old sheep is a twin of this
old one, and they are so fond of each
other that we cannot keep them separate. At first we were afraid the aunty
would injure the young ones, and we
shut her out in the barn-yard, but she
came and stood at the door, there by
the wagon, and cried so piteously that
Mr. Brooks told me she might stay in
with her sister and her baby nieces. We
could not bear to hear her bleat so."

"Don't she bite or tread on them?" asked Bessie.

"No," said Martin, "I think she is very tender with them. This morning one of the men threw a handful of hay accidentally in a lamb's face, and when it tried to push it off but couldn't, what does old aunty do but walk up and eat it away, every whisp. I thought that was quite bright of her, and kind too. On the whole I think they are a happy family."

"Does Nelly like 'em?" asked Bessie, as she patted the head of the one Martin called the "aunty."

"Yes," said Martin, "she thinks they are the handsomest animals on the place. They grow fonder of her every day."

"I hope her father don't mean to have

them killed," remarked Bessie, a little sadly.

"No indeed," cried Martin, "he bought them for pets, and to look pretty running about the meadow in the summer time. He says they are too tame and loving to be killed. I shouldn't like to think of such a thing, I am sure. There, — do see old Moolly poking her head over the wagon! How she does want to come in! She always was our pet before, and I suppose it makes her a little jealous. Poor Moolly, — good little Moolly."

Martin picked up a corn-cob and rubbed the cow's ears. She stood quite still to let him do it, and when he stopped she stretched out her head for more and looked at him as if she had not had half her share.

"Are the little lambs named?" asked Bessie, as she got up from the hay to go.

"No," said Martin; "Nelly's father told her she might call them any thing she wanted, but she thinks they are such funny little long-legged things that she cannot find names pretty enough. When they grow stronger they will frisk about and be full. of play."

"I mean to run over to the house to see her and ask her about it," said Bessie. "I am real glad you called me, Martin, to look at them."

Martin went back to his hay-cutting, and Bessie bade him good-by, and skipped along the path to the house. Bessie always skipped instead of walking or running, when she was particularly pleased with any thing. On knocking at the farm-house door, she was told to her great sorrow that Nelly was not within, but when she heard that she had just started to pay a visit to herself, that sorrow was changed to joy, and she turned to go home with a very light heart and a pair of very brisk feet.

"Perhaps I can overtake her," she said to herself; but go as fast as she could, she saw nothing of Nelly on the road. When she reached home, she was so warm with the exercise that it seemed to her as though the day were a very mild one indeed. As she pushed open the door of the kitchen, her eyes were so bright and her cheeks so red from her little run, that her mother looked up from her work and asked what she had been doing.

"Only racing down the hill to find Nelly," panted Bessie, sinking into a chair as she spoke. "Isn't she here? I didn't overtake her."

"No," replied her mother, "Nelly has been here and gone. She was sorry you were out."

"Gone!" echoed Bessie. "Well, if that is not too bad! Mrs. Brooks said she had just started. I am so sorry. Did she tell you which way she was going?"

"No," said her mother, "she did not, but she said perhaps she would stop on her way back. Come, take off your hat and shawl and hang them up, and then begin hemming one of these towels. I am in a great hurry to get them done. They are Mrs. Raynor's, and I promised to send them home to-morrow."

Bessie loved to romp and play much better than to sew, and these words of her mother's did not consequently fill her with satisfaction. She knew, however, that by sewing their living was to be gained, so she choked down the fretful words that rose to her lips. She felt that it was hard enough for her mother to work, without having her repinings to endure also. The glow and cheerful effect of her walk, however, faded away as she slowly untied her hood, and hung it with her shawl on a peg behind the door. She was deeply disappointed at Nelly's absence.

"I wish she would have waited a little while," she said; "I don't see her so often now the winter has set in, that I can afford to miss her. Mother, have you seen my thimble?"

"What!" said her mother, "lost *again*, Bessie? What shall I do with this careless girl? There is my old one, you can use that for a little while."

"Oh, now I remember," cried Bessie, springing up, "I left it in the garret, in the drawer of the old table, the last time I was there. I'll get it, and be down again in a moment."

She opened the door at the foot of the stairs, and ran quickly up them. She did not notice that she left the door wide open, and that the cold air rushed into the warm kitchen, nor did she know that her mother, sighing, was obliged to rise from her work and shut it after her.

On went Bessie, and turning the landing, began the second flight, two steps at a time, as usual. She was very light-footed, and owing to her disappointment about Nelly, she did not feel quite gay enough to hum the little tunes which she generally did when going about the house, so that altogether she scarcely made any noise. Perhaps it was owing to this that, as she reached the head of the garret stairs, she saw something run across the floor, evidently alarmed at her unexpected appearance. She stood still for a moment, hardly knowing what it was, and not wishing to go any further in the fear of frightening it away before she could get a good look at it. She decided at once, however, from its size, that it was not a rat, for it was far too large. It had taken refuge behind some old furniture in a corner, and in the hope that if she kept perfectly still, it would venture out again,

she sat down on the top step, and fixed
her eyes intently on the spot where she
had beheld it disappear. She had remained thus but a short time when she
heard hasty footsteps coming from the
kitchen, and a voice that she recognized as that of Nelly, called her name.
She did not answer, for she wanted to
unravel the mystery, whatever it might
be, and when Nelly, still calling, followed
her up to the stairs on which she sat,
she put her finger on her lip by way
of enjoining silence, and beckoned to
her to come to her. Nelly understood
in a moment, and slipping off her heavy
winter walking shoes, crept up and sat
down beside her.

"Hush!" whispered Bessie, "don't
make a sound. There is some sort of
a little animal concealed behind that

old fire-board, and I want to see it come out."

She spoke so low that Nelly had difficulty in getting at the sense of what she said, but when she did, she nodded slightly, and the two little girls began the watch together.

They sat there a long, long time.

Once or twice they thought they heard a movement behind the fire-board, but they saw nothing. At last, just as they were becoming very weary of remaining so long in the cold, Nelly caught sight of a small pointed nose, projecting from one side of the board. As this nose moved slowly forward, a pair of bright little eyes came into view also, rolling restlessly about, as if seeking to espy danger. It was with difficulty the children could repress the exclamations that were on their lips, but with an effort they did so, and remained just as quiet as before. Encouraged by the dead stillness, the animal advanced still further from its retreat, peering all the while about it. Its body, as near as they could see, was spotted gray and white, and so were its pretty ears, which were long, and in constant motion. It ran cautiously from its place of concealment, and at last, with a graceful, hurried spring, landed on the top of Bessie's table. Arrived there, it sat down and looked about it again. The children did not move. The drawer of the table, as usual, was partially open, according to Bessie's careless habit, and the little creature put its mites of paws carefully in the crack, bringing them

out again almost immediately with a
nut, at which at once it commenced to
nibble. It was an odd sight as it sat
there on its hind legs, holding the nut
in its front paws, and twisting and turning it from side to side in order to find
a good place to plant its sharp teeth.
Nelly glanced at Bessie and longed to
burst into a laugh, but Bessie signified
to her by a movement of her eye-brows
and lips that she must not. It was
plain enough by this time that the little
thief was a squirrel. Bessie was quite
bewildered at the thought that it had
been able to get in the house without
her or her mother's knowledge. She
did not know that the race to which
the animal belonged is proverbial for
its cunning, and that often it steals a

way into the habitations of men for no other purpose than to find seeds and grains on which to live.

Some accidental movement which Bessie made, at length startled the squirrel from its sense of security. It leaped lightly from the table to the floor, and disappeared behind some loose blocks of wood, near the fire-board. As it did so, Nelly saw that part of its tail was missing, looking as if torn off at about half its length.

"Bessie!" she exclaimed eagerly, as her companion made a dart for the blocks of wood, "Bessie, as sure as you're alive, that's the same squirrel we saw in the woods, the day we went nutting."

"I know it," cried Bessie; "at least

I am as sure as I can be, for that one was like this, spotted white and gray, and each of them had only a part of a tail. To think of the little thing being so hungry as to come after my nuts! If I can only find its hole, I'll feed it regularly every day."

"What *could* bring it so far from the woods?" cried Nelly, laughing. "I never heard of any thing more strange, even in a book."

"You stay here and watch if it comes out again," said Bessie, "and I'll run tell mother. Perhaps she can help find its hiding-place."

Nelly went with her as far as the foot of the stairs to get her shoes, for her feet were now growing very cold. Then she returned to the garret, but

nothing more had been seen of the
squirrel when Bessie appeared with her
mother.

"It was here, just here, that it went
out of sight," cried Bessie; "somewhere
by these blocks and this old fire-board."

Her mother laughed, and said if there
were nothing worse than a squirrel in
the house, she should be glad.

"We must look," she added, "and
perhaps we can discover its nest; that
is, if it has one here, for, Bessie, it has
just occurred to me that this is the
way your Madeira nut disappeared. If
we can find the nest we may find your
money too," and she began to move out
the furniture from the wall.

At the mention of the Madeira nut,
Bessie colored deeply, and really seemed
struck with true shame.

"Oh, mother," she said, "to think that I have never, all this while, cleaned out that drawer! Some of the nuts are still in it, and the other things too, just as they were that day when I lost my money. I have meant to clear it out so many times!"

Her mother turned and looked at her sorrowfully.

"Bessie," she said, "I have for years done all I could do, to make a careful, neat little girl, out of a careless, untidy one. I am beginning now to leave you to yourself, hoping that time will help you to see yourself as others see you. I have noticed often that your drawer remained in the same condition, but I did not speak of it."

"Oh, mother," cried Bessie, frightened, "don't leave me to myself, *don't*. I shall never learn to be good at all, that way. Oh, don't give me up yet."

"My poor child," said her mother, "if you will only *try*, so that I can *see* you trying, my confidence in you will come back, but not otherwise. I want something more than empty promises. You forget them as soon as you make them."

"But I will try, I will *really* try *this* time," said Bessie with tears in her eyes. "I'm *lazy*, mother, I'm *real* lazy, but I am not as bad as I might be. I'll clean the drawer just as soon as we look for the nest, *sure*."

"Well," said her mother, half smiling at the little girl's doleful tone, "well, I will give you this one more chance. We will take the drawer for a new starting point. Come, Nelly, let us search now for the squirrel's hole. It must be somewhere about here, for it would never come up by the stairs, I think."

They began a thorough hunt, lifting up every light article in the out-garret, where they were, and dragging the more ponderous furniture from their places. It was a sort of store-away place for things not in every-day use, and therefore it took some time to examine every thing. An occasional pile of nibbled nut-shells was all that was brought to light.

"Well," said Nelly, laughing, as she looked under the last article, a little broken chair belonging to Bessie. "Well, I don't see but that Madame Squirrel has escaped us. I can't meet with a trace of her, for my part, beyond these nut-shells."

"Nor I either," wofully added Bessie.

"Yet how could it have run away from us, since we can find no hole in the floor, and Nelly did not see it run into any of these other rooms?" asked Bessie's mother.

"Perhaps it is hidden in the furniture itself," remarked Nelly.

"Stop a moment," said Bessie's mother, as Nelly began to pull out the drawers of an old bureau, "here are some cross-beams in the wall by the fire-board, that look very much as though a set of sharp teeth had nibbled a hole in them, — yes, it is so! Well, I think we've tracked the squirrel now! The place is such a little way from the floor, that it could jump in and scamper off through the walls, before any one could molest it. Perhaps it is far away in the woods, laughing at us, at this minute."

The children drew near the beams in
question, with strong curiosity. It was
indeed as Bessie's mother said; there
were the marks of teeth in the wood,
and just where the beams joined was
a hole quite large enough for a squirrel
to pass through.

"It is the same one we saw in the
woods, I know it is," said Nelly, "but
what should bring it here?"

"Perhaps, in time, we can tame it;
that is if we have not already frightened
it away. *May* I try to tame it, mother?"

"Yes," said her mother. "I think Bunny will make a pretty pet. We can
strew a few grains of corn, or a few
nuts about its hole every day, until it
learns to regard us as its friends; but
a little girl that I know must get into
the good habit of putting her things in

their proper places, and shutting her table drawers *tight*, or it will continue to help itself to more valuable things, and make itself a plague to us. I do not doubt that Bunny has your money in its nest at this minute. It thought, probably, that it was carrying off a good, sound nut."

"Yes," said Bessie, "and I dare say it was it that ran off with those in my basket, and all the others in the garden. Poor, dear Nathan! I must tell him about it, and ask him to forget my cross words. One of my Sunday-school hymns says, 'Kind words can never die.' I wonder if the unkind words live forever too. Do they, mother?"

"I hope not," was the answer, "but many an unkind word leaves a sting in the mind of the person to whom it is said, long after the one who uttered it has entirely forgotten it. I don't believe Nathan, for instance, will soon cease to remember that you asked him why he took your nuts. You acted too impulsively."

"Too *what*, mother?" asked Bessie, curiously.

"Too *impulsively*. That is, you did not wait to consider the matter, but spoke out just as you felt, as soon as you saw him. You must certainly ask him to excuse you. If you are always very gentle to him in future, perhaps your offence will be forgotten. There is no end to the soothing effect of those 'kind words that never die!'"

"He was cross enough with *me* about

it," said Bessie, reflectively. "I think a few kind words would not hurt *him* to say."

"We have nothing to do with Nathan as to that," said her mother. "If he chooses to be ill-tempered, it is his own business, while it is ours to bear it from him patiently. It is only by such means that we can teach him how wrong he is."

"I think that is pretty hard to do," said Bessie, shaking her head, "don't you, Nelly? *I* always want to answer right straight back."

"And if you do," said her mother, "you will find that you invariably make the case worse than before. A noble poet, whose works you may read when you are older, has said, 'Be silent and endure!' and experience will prove to you both, that this silence and this endurance is the true key to happiness. Now, run down stairs, Bessie, and bring me up the little saw. The idea has just come to me, to saw away some of the board at the side of these beams. That will give us a good view of what is going on in the wall, and will not hurt its appearance much, either."

Bessie soon reappeared with the saw, which, as it was small, her mother had no difficulty in handling. She took it from her and began operations at once, inserting the sharp end of it in a crevice in the wood, and moving it gradually across the grain, until the end of the board fell on the floor, where the saw-dust already lay.

"Oh, let me see!" cried Bessie, in wild delight at this exposure of the squirrel's haunt. And

"Oh, let *me* see *too!*" cried Nelly.

But Bessie's mother said she thought she had better take a peep first, so she lowered her eyes to the aperture and looked in. It was dark, and her eyes, accustomed to the sun-light, at first could distinguish nothing. Gradually, however, she found that she could see a little way around the hole with great distinctness, and it was not long before a small heap of rags, apparently, attracted her attention on one of the corner beams.

"What is it, mother? what do you find?" cried Bessie, as her mother put in her hand to feel what this heap could be. Something warm met the touch of her fingers, and she drew back, slightly startled.

On examining further, she found that this was indeed the animal's nest, and that these soft, warm objects, curled up in it so nicely, were probably her little young ones.

"There!" she said, laughing, "come see, children, what I have found! Here is the squirrel's nest, and two of her little babies!"

The girls peered eagerly through the hole at these newly discovered treasures.

"The darlings!" cried Bessie, "we can surely tame these little creatures, mother, they are so young. It will be no trouble at all."

"We must not take them from the nest," replied her mother. "If we can tame them by kindness, and by gradually accustoming them to our harmless visits, I am very willing to make pets of them."

"Oh, how pleasant that will be," exclaimed Bessie, in an ecstasy. " Do look, Nelly, at their pretty eyes. I don't know but that I shall be just as well satisfied with my two little squirrels as you are with your two lambs."

As she spoke, she put in her hand to touch the tiny animals on the head, and smooth them softly, but something at the side of the nest suddenly arrested her attention, and she did not do so.

" Oh, mother," she cried, " I do believe here is my Madeira nut, among this rubbish and empty hickory shells about the nest. I do believe it, — I do believe it! It *looks* like it, I am positive of that. It seems whole, too. I don't think it has been nibbled at all! How glad I am!"

"Can you reach it?" asked her mother; "if you can, do so."

Bessie made what she called "a long arm," and in a moment more she seized the nut and brought it into open daylight.

"Oh, mother," she said, dancing around the garret joyfully, "it *is* my nut! Here is a little place in the side where the squirrel has bitten, and you can see the money right through it! She found that there was nothing good to eat in it, so she stopped just in time not to spoil it entirely. I am so glad — I am so glad!"

THE END.